Flying faster and FASTER...

All Rights Reserved. No reproduction, copy or transmission of the publication may be made without written permission. No paragraph or section of this publication may be reproduced copied or transmitted save with the written permission or in accordance with the provisions of the Copyright Act 1956 (as amended).
Copyright 2017 Kellie Hamill. The right of Kellie Hamill to be identified as the author of this work has been asserted in accordance with the Copyright Designs and Patents Act 1988. A copy of this book is deposited with the British Library

Published by
i2i Publishing. Manchester.
http://www.i2ipublishing.co.uk